Hello, Family Members,

Learning to read is one of the most important accomplishments of early childhood. **Hello Reader!** books are designed to help children become skilled readers who like to read. Beginning readers learn to read by remembering frequently used words like "the," "is," and "and"; by using phonics skills to decode new words; and by interpreting picture and text clues. These books provide both the stories children enjoy and the structure they need to read fluently and independently. Here are suggestions for helping your child *before, during,* and *after* reading:

Before

- Look at the cover and pictures and have your child predict what the story is about.
- Read the story to your child.
- Encourage your child to chime in with familiar words and phrases.
- Echo read with your child by reading a line first and having your child read it after you do.

During

- Have your child think about a word he or she does not recognize right away. Provide hints such as "Let's see if we know the sounds" and "Have we read other words like this one?"
- Encourage your child to use phonics skills to sound out new words.
- Provide the word for your child when more assistance is needed so that he or she does not struggle and the experience of reading with you is a positive one.
- Encourage your child to have fun by reading with a lot of expression . . . like an actor!

After

- Have your child keep lists of interesting and favorite words.
- Encourage your child to read the books over and over again. Have him or her read to brothers, sisters, grandparents, and even teddy bears. Repeated readings develop confidence in young readers.
- Talk about the stories. Ask and answer questions. Share ideas about the funniest and most interesting characters and events in the stories.

I do hope that you and your child enjoy this book.

—Francie Alexander
Reading Specialist,
Scholastic's Learning Ventures

P9-CFU-830

For Basia — one to grow on
—M.S.

For my two great friends,
Lucinda and Maryann
—K.B.

No part of this publication may be reproduced, or stored in a retrieval system, or transmitted in any form or by any means, electronic, mechanical, photocopying, recording, or otherwise, without written permission of the publisher. For information regarding permissions, write to Scholastic Inc., Attention: Permissions Department, 555 Broadway, New York, NY 10012.

Text copyright © 1999 by Mary Serfozo.
Illustrations copyright © 1999 by Katy Bratun.
All rights reserved. Published by Scholastic Inc.
SCHOLASTIC, HELLO READER, CARTWHEEL BOOKS and associated logos
are trademarks and/or registered trademarks of Scholastic Inc.

Library of Congress Cataloging-in-Publication

Serfozo, Mary.
    A head is for hats / by Mary Serfozo; illustrated by Katy Bratun.
        p.   cm.—(Hello reader! Level 2)
    "Cartwheel Books."
    Summary: Rhyming text describes parts of the body and their uses—
hands for waving and painting, a mouth for singing and eating—and tells how
the parts add up to be a unique person.
    ISBN 0-439-09909-9
    [1. Body, Human—Fiction.   2. Identity—Fiction.   3. Stories in rhyme.]
    I. Bratun, Katy, ill.   II. Title.   III. Series.
    PZ8.3.S4688He 1999
    [E]—dc21   99-31959
                                                                          CIP

12   11   10   9   8   7   6   5   4   0/0 01 02 03 04

Printed in the U.S.A.   24
First printing, October 1999

A Head Is for Hats

by Mary Serfozo
Illustrated by Katy Bratun

Hello Reader! — Level 2

SCHOLASTIC INC.
Cartwheel ·B·O·O·K·S·®

New York Toronto London Auckland Sydney
Mexico City New Delhi Hong Kong

A head is for hats
and for holding your hair
and for all of the thoughts
that you think inside there.

An ear on each side,
set in just the right place,

keeps your hat safe from sliding
down over your face.

Your ears are for hearing
a whisper or shout

or a squeak,
squawk,
or honk—
any sound
that's about.

Your eyes are for looking
and seeing and spying,

for reading your writing,
and just maybe—
for crying.

The nose in between
can smell cookies and cakes

or a skunk in your bunk.
What a difference that makes!

A mouth may be busy
with speaking or eating,

with singing and cheering
or grinning and greeting.

Your hands are for touching

and painting and drawing,

for working and waving

and pounding and sawing.

While feet are for standing
and stamping and stomping

and racing and chasing
and clomping and romping.

And that's how it goes
from your nose to your toes.

But is that all there is?
NO!

As everyone knows,

in between there's a body
with arms and legs, too.

When you add it all up,
then it comes out to . . .

YOU!